The Tails of Victoria Way

Angela Howells

AuthorHouse™ UK Ltd.
500 Avebury Boulevard
Central Milton Keynes, MK9 2BE
www.authorhouse.co.uk
Phone: 08001974150

© 2009 Angela Howells. All rights reserved.

No part of this book may be reproduced, stored in a retrieval system, or transmitted by any means without the written permission of the author.

First published by AuthorHouse   11/13/2009

ISBN: 978-1-4490-4432-9 (sc)

Printed in the United States of America
Bloomington, Indiana

This book is printed on acid-free paper.

authorHOUSE®

This book is dedicated to all the wonderful kids in my life, without whom, this book would not have been possible:

My four big kids, Layla, Dale Kristian & Lee
My adorable grandchildren, Ellis & Kyle
My three lovable rogues, Jacob, Darren and David
And the special kid in my life Ethan
Finally, to 'Wally' my husband, the biggest kid of all!
Somehow he 'worms' his way into everything!!
With much love xxx

Contents

Chapter 1
Homeless 1

Chapter 2
A New Beginning 2

Chapter 3
Making Friends 5

Chapter 4
Forget Me Nut Squirrel 8

Chapter 5
Maggie The Magpie 10

Chapter 6
The Invisible cockerel 12

Chapter 7
D I Hopper 15

Chapter 8
Barn a bee 18

Chapter 9
A Special Bond 20

Chapter 10
The Expedition 22

Chapter 11
The Lost Quail 23

Chapter 12
Time For Bed 26

Chapter 1
HOMELESS

Wally worm awoke with a start!! "What was that?! Am I dreaming?"
There was a loud roar of an engine and Wally felt himself being lifted into the air.

"What's happening to me?!" He gasped, "Worms don't fly!" Suddenly and with a jolt, Wally was flung to the ground. He lay still until the sound of the angry engine, faded into the distance. Bravely he wriggled through the mud, and poked his head up, like a periscope. The realisation of what was happening to him began to sink in.

Wally lived in the garden of number 3 Victoria Way. The owner Mikey was having a conservatory installed at the rear of the property, which meant the area had to be excavated. All of the cool, firm mud, which was once Wally's home, was being thrown out at the front of the property by a large digger. Wally felt powerless as his home was clawed at, piece by piece, by that great big ugly yellow monster of a digger! Sighing, he knew if he stayed he wouldn't be safe. As quick as he could, he wriggled out of the mud and lay on top of a mound, whilst he considered his plan.

He pondered, a little concerned at what lay ahead. A large tarmacadam drive and courtyard which led to numbers 1 & 2 or a short wiggle next door to number 4. Wally had always wondered what it would be like living in the 'big house' number 1, with the huge garden, and as if fate had stepped in, it was now his chance to seize the opportunity.

Victoria Way was a new development set in an old coaching town of Coleshill, Warwickshire, England. Although the properties were newly built, the design was well in keeping with the character of the town.

There were two, three storey high semi detached houses and two bungalows, set behind large security gates. A quiet development, - well most of the time, until the three boys who lived at number 1 came out to play on their bikes! They were always laughing, so life at number 1 must be good fun. It was decided.

"I will move into number 1" said Wally worm excitedly, but with a little apprehension too. He wiggled down from the mound and set off on the start of a new adventure.

Chapter 2
A New Beginning

Wally set off. The tarmac surface felt rough on his skin and he didn't seem to move as quickly as he could through the mud. It was a damp, grey morning, worms like cool surfaces, he was so glad it wasn't hot.

Very soon Wally mastered his wiggles, and picked up 'worms pace' across the drive. It was exhausting!

A small puddle was a welcome opportunity to freshen up, quench one's thirst, and continue on the journey to No 1.

Fortunately worms are quite resourceful. Wally didn't need any suitcases or belongings, worms just survive from day to day. Besides, how could he carry a suitcase anyway? Worms don't have arms or hands to carry anything!!

Although it was sad leaving what was once Wally's home, there is always something new and exciting around the corner…..

Screech!!!

"What on earth was that!!" gasped Wally.

He jumped up, wow! A great big monster truck just missed him, with its gigantic wheels!

With large letters of a tyre company stamped across them. POLNUD.

Wally wouldn't want those letters imprinted on his body!! Not that he could read them! You need eyes for that! But somehow he sensed the danger.

(Wally was soon to learn that those monster trucks were called 4 x 4's).

"That was close!" said Wally, as he wiggled closer to two garages situated in the courtyard.

"Looks as if the 'huge mans' (humans) have left for a while, so i should be safe now".

Wally's tummy began to rumble, he was hungry. Up periscope. He lifted his head and sensed what was around him. Beside the garages was a very green and lush area. "Lunch" muttered Wally. He slithered through the long grass and mouched around until finally settling on a leafy lunch. Although Wally felt full and wanted an afternoon nap, he knew he had to keep moving onwards, his new home was just a short distance away.

Wally discovered the surface near the garages was much smoother than the tarmac and he seemed to wiggle along with ease. Suddenly! A large blackbird swooped down and landed right in front of him. Startled! Wally remembered what his mother had always taught him.

"Stay away from those flying beasts - they will want to eat you. Use all of your senses, you may not be able to see them but you will know how to avoid danger!"

"Gulp," said Wally as he swallowed hard.

Whoosh another blackbird appeared!

Wally rolled backwards and wedged himself under a small ledge.

"Well, did you get him!" said the blackbird.

"No, did you?" replied his accomplice.

"Are you sure? Open your beak, let me see!" Insisted the first blackbird.

"No I did not! Open your beak let me see!! I bet you got him, you just don't want to share..."

The birds continued squabbling until they became bored, then they began to gossip about what was happening at number 3, and soon forgot what they were arguing about in the first place! They finally decided to swoop into number 2, to see if they could find any scraps. Once it was safe, Wally rolled out from under the ledge.

Wally had never had so many near misses in such a short time before; it was enough to give him a 'worm attack!'

Determined, he wiggled on faster than ever, and at last there he was positioned at the bottom of a large wooden gate and guess what??

It was locked!!

"Oh help!" said Wally.

"I travelled all this way and I can't get in"

For the first time he felt quite despondent.

"What am i thinking?" Rationalised Wally,

"I can't go over it, I'm a worm! I can go under it. I wonder what is on the other side?"

Wally decided it would be safer to squeeze under the gap at the bottom of the fence. Cautiously, he wriggled underneath. He met with another big wooden monstrosity, but managed to weave his way around it.

Finally, there was everything he always dreamed of, the huge garden of number 1, the big house!

He burrowed his way into the soft earth and settled down for the night.

Tomorrow is just the beginning of his new life at number 1 Victoria Way.

Chapter 3
MAKING FRIENDS

"Onwards and upwards!" said a voice.

"Who's that?" Wondered Wally as he munched on a leaf. There stood a most unusual creature. Wally had never encountered such a thing before. He had a small head with 'things' sticking up and a hard round object on his back. "Hello" said Wally, as he accidently bumped into him.

"Sorry, I often bump into things. When I was little, mum could never tell me to look where I was going! Worms can't see you know!"

The creature laughed!

"Good morning, you're new around here aren't you?"

"Yes" said Wally, "moved in last night, my name's Wally worm".

"Very pleased to meet you. I'm Sir Hillary Cling On."

"He must be important if he's a Sir," thought Wally.

"I hope you don't mind my saying," advised Wally, "but I think you have something stuck to your back?"

Wally was quite close to him and could feel something rather odd.

"My house," replied Sir Hillary.

"Your house!" Remarked Wally, believing he must be amazingly strong to carry such a thing.

"Yes, my house, I have shelter wherever I go, very useful you know."

"Have you got any windows?" Queried Wally.

"I don't have any windows," laughed Sir Hillary.

"Well, have you got any stairs?"

"No, I don't need any stairs." Sir Hillary found Wally most amusing.

"It must be like a moving bungalow?" Thought Wally.

"Do you have a door?" Wally continued, he was most inquisitive.

"Of course i have a door!"

With that Sir Hillary's head disappeared! Total silence.

"He's a magician!" Said Wally. "He's gone."

"Hello, are you there?"

Quite unexpectedly Sir Hillary's head shot out.

"Boo!!!" He roared.

"Oh wow," said Wally "I've never experienced anything quite like this before!"

He was amazed.

"Now if you don't mind, I am trying to reach that post on the fence. My first challenge of the day. Onwards and upwards."

"One last question if you don't mind Sir." He continued.

"There appears to be something noisy coming from your house?" Wally could hear a whistling sound.

"Have you left the kettle on?"

Sir Hillary chuckled. "Kettle on!"

"That's my hearing aid, Wally. Can't hear a damn thing without it!" He cursed.

Wally stood silently as Sir Hillary Cling On, very slowly trudged along, sticking bit by bit, and clinging on to the fence. After what appeared to be hours, he succeeded.

"Hooray!" shouted Sir Hillary.

"Well done," congratulated Wally. Hadn't got a clue what he'd done, but egged him on all the same.

Wally soon learned that Sir Hillary Cling On was named after a great expeditionist, the first man to climb Mount Everest, Sir Edmund Hillary.

Sir Hillary Cling On became knighted after successfully climbing the second leg of the barbecue! However, he advised that you never go any higher. You never know if the owners are French? Sir Hillary is a snail and according to tradition 'snails' are a delicacy to the French so they may decide to cook him!

"Escargot," he informed Wally. "We snails go into hiding on the 24th May! National Escargot Day!!!"

"Yuk!" Thought Wally. "It didn't bear thinking about. Deep fried snail!!"

This was Wally's first real friend. He would cheer Sir Hillary on in all of his adventures. On one occasion, Wally cheered excitedly, as Sir Hillary reached the top of the step to the French doors. (Ooh that word 'French' again. Just the thought of that word sent a shiver down Wally's tail).

Suddenly! One of the 'huge mans' opened the door, and sent him hurtling backwards! Sir Hillary landed with a crash and a squelch. Then there was deadly silence.

"Sir Hillary!" Yelled Wally.

"Are you hurt?"

Not a sound.

"Oh no!" said Wally sadly. "He must be dead."

Suddenly, "Boo!! Thought I was a gonna didn't you, just a little shell shocked! Never mind, onwards and upwards…"

Wally began to realise just how brave Sir Hillary Cling On really was. That shell of his protected him from wind, rain, sun and of course those French doors!

(Ooh that word French again!)

Wally and Sir Hillary became the greatest of friends and would always look out for each other. Wally was so glad he'd moved to number 1 or he may never have met him.

Wally's mum always told him 'remember, something good always comes out of a bad situation'. And she was right.

Chapter 4
FORGET ME NUT SQUIRREL

"Tut, Tut"

"Tut, Tut"

"If only I could remember, where I buried that nut?"

There stood this furry creature, grey in colour with a huge bushy tail. She busied herself and seldom stood still.

"Who's that?" Wally asked Sir Hillary.

"That's a squirrel," Sir Hillary replied. "Rumour has it; she fell out of a tree and banged her head."

"How tragic," said Wally.

"Since then, she can't remember her name, or where she lives," Sir Hillary advised.

"That's how she got the name 'Forget me nut.' Can't seem to remember where she's buried her nuts."

"It's a wonder she survives, but somehow she does…..always seems to have a good supply."

Just then, those two spiteful gossiping blackbirds swooped in!

"Quick hide Wally," warned Sir Hillary.

Sir Hillary's head darted into his shell and he shut his door!

Wally buried himself in the mud.

Those two pesky birds had only one thing on their minds, to tease 'Forget me nut' squirrel.

"Forget me nut, Forget me nut, is out of her tree and totally nuts!!" Teased the blackbirds.

Then they swooped off to number 4. Sir Hillary's head popped out.

"Coast clear Wally, they've gone."

"Why are they so mean to everyone?" Asked Wally sadly.

"Take no notice of them," reassured Sir Hillary, "They have nothing better to do all day but swoop in, and mind everybody's business, you'll get used to them. They always gossip, that's why they were named 'Tittle and Tattle.'

"What perfect names," laughed Wally.

"And as far as Forget me nut is concerned….." said Sir Hillary laughing.

"She can't remember anything they say to her, so it doesn't bother her one bit! The last laugh is always on them!

Wally and Sir Hillary laughed.

"Silly birds!"

Wally followed Sir Hillary as he looked around the garden and went in search of his next expedition.

Chapter 5
MAGGIE THE MAGPIE

Wally worm admired 'Forget me nut' squirrel, as she busied herself dashing up and down trees, scooting across the garden.

"Does she ever stop?" Wally asked.

"Her pace of life is very different to ours," informed Sir Hillary. "Our life is much slower down here on the ground."

"Isn't it sad she has no home," Wally empathised.

"No not at all. Believe me, Forget me nut is truly happy."

Replied Sir Hillary. "Way up above are many trees? A chain of hotels, 'The Tree Top Hotels.' Forget me nut stops in a different hotel everyday. No need for housekeeping or cleaning and that keeps Maggie really happy, and never out of work!"

"Who's Maggie?" Questioned Wally.

"Maggie the Magpie of course! She's the housekeeper providing a maid service for all the hotels. Always tidying and cleaning, those branches are spotless!"

And there she was, perched on a branch, looking crisp in a uniform of blue, white and yellow. Perfectly turned out.

"She must be beautiful." Whispered Wally dreamily.

"Yes but remember, worms and flying beasts don't get along!" Said Sir Hillary.

"Oh, yes uh uh!" Coughed Wally.

That brought Wally back to reality, quite quickly!!

Sir Hillary chuckled as he explained to Wally worm how Maggie always thinks she's done an exceptional job as Forget me nut always leaves her lots of tips — nuts!!

Maggie doesn't realise that Forget me nut leaves them behind because she forgets where she's left them!

"So you see Wally, everyone's happy."

Wally agreed! It's true something good always seems to happen.

Chapter 6
THE INVISIBLE COCKEREL

"Cocka doodle doo
Cocka doodle dee
I make a lot of noise
But you can't see me".

"What on earth was that?!" Wally awoke startled!

Sir Hillary popped his head out of his shell.

"Morning Wally, oh that! That's the Invisible Cockerel!"

"He always makes a lot of noise — you can hear him but nobody has ever seen him, rumour is he's invisible!"

"Invisible!!" Wally was shocked and looked quite nervous. (Not that Wally could see him even if he wanted too).

Don't worry Wally, he has never hurt anyone, but he can be quite annoying. His time clock is not always set right!

He's supposed to wake us up, sometimes it's 04.30am!! When I'm unwinding. Sometimes the afternoon when I'm trying to sleep! Sometimes it's evening when I'm raring to go!"

"Frustrating thing is, you can't throw anything at him to shut him up, because you can't see him!" Laughed Sir Hillary.

"So, we have to put up with him. Have you ever heard of such a thing? A cockerel who doesn't know what time of the day it is!! Could only happen at Victoria Way, that's for sure!!"

Wally laughed. Sure enough, life here at Victoria Way, there never was a dull moment!

"Well, is it morning then?" Asked Wally worm.

"Oh yes! Ironically, he seems to be on time today." They both laughed.

The sun began to shine, and then quite unexpectedly the French doors were flung open.

(Ooh! That word French again!)

"What a din!! Who needs a cockerel with that noisy lot!" Thought Wally.

It was the three boys from number 1. And two more! Five noisy kids!! Jacob, Darren, David, Ellis and Kyle.

> COCKADOODLE DOO COCKADOODLE DEE. I MAKE A LOT OF NOISE, BUT YOU CAN'T SEE ME

The boys raced across the garden and kicked this great big round object, which had a bears face on it, straight towards Wally and Sir Hillary!!

"Take Cover!!" Shouted Sir Hillary.

Wally didn't waste a second. He burrowed into the ground in an instant.

"What was that? Can you hear me??" Wally whispered.

"Yes, I can hear you, and that is called a ball, and they sure hurt!"

Wally could hear a rumbling sound from the earth above him. The kids were in some sort of car, where they have to use their feet to move it.

"How odd?" Thought Wally.

Wally listened to what was happening above him.

The kids squealed and screamed and ran across the garden. They laughed and argued as most kids do. That Jacob was the worst, the oldest, always bossing everyone around and telling everyone what to do!

"No Darren ! No David!.........

As for Darren, he must have two left feet! He falls over everything and everyone and nothing at all! Just like Mr Tumble!!

"Bang, Bump, Bang......"

Then there's David. 'Cough, Cough, Cough. Rattle, rattle, rattle. Wheeze! They call him 'Wheezy'. The 'Huge mans' put a large plastic contraption on his face and tell him to breathe, as they squirt smoke into his mouth!

"Yuk!" Thought Wally. "Why would anyone want to squirt smoke into his mouth?"

Then there's Ellis. Thinks he's a super hero, pretends to fight off the enemy and save the day!! Jumps everywhere! His feet must be fitted with springs!! Sir Hillary advised you're not that safe when he's around!!

Now Kyle, he's the cute one, the toddler, but very much like Sir Hillary, very adventurous! He is always looking for a new challenge. Suddenly, the huge man could be heard shouting……

"No!! Be careful!! Get down from there!!"

"Aaaah!!" He screamed. "Boo hoo, sob sob!!"

The huge man put a cold compress on his head and Kyle could be heard crying and screaming.

"And who could blame him!" Thought Wally. "Sir Hillary wouldn't want anyone interfering with his expeditions!

How could you achieve your goals if you were constantly interrupted? How would Kyle ever get knighted at this rate?"

Soon there was silence. All the kids ran indoors. (Yes those French ones — Ooh!)

Peace and quiet at last! Wally and Sir Hillary settled down for an afternoon nap!!

Chapter 7
D I Hopper

"Cockadoodle doo, Cockadoodle dee,
I make a lot of noise,
But you can't see me."

"That pesky cockerel again!! His time clock is all wrong, it's the middle of the afternoon!" Groaned Sir Hillary. "And I'm trying to sleep!"

"Oh well," he continued, "onwards and upwards."

He set off towards the children's playhouse which had a large mesh frontage; he hadn't attempted to climb that before.

Just as he was about to get started, the excited sound of kids voices could be heard from next door number 2.

Sir Hillary looked up.

"Whee! Whee!"

A little girl's face appeared over the fence, then she disappeared. Then she appeared again.

"Whee! Whee!"

15

Then a little boy appeared, then he disappeared.

"What's happening?" Wally was bewildered. Sir Hillary explained.

Wally thought the kids next door could actually fly!! (He didn't realise they were bouncing on a trampoline).

Wally loved the sound of laughter. It was certainly an experience living here at number 1.

Quite unexpectedly, this strange looking creature appeared.

He had six legs and his back was green and black, he looked like a leaf. Sir Hillary described him to Wally.

"What a great disguise!" Thought Wally.

He would fly quite low and occasionally hop. He blended in with the leaves, which concealed his identity. He spoke to Sir Hillary.

"Sir Hillary, did you see or hear anything out of the ordinary last night approximately 23.00 hours."

"No, can't say I did," he replied, "why what's wrong?"

Wally soon discovered this creature that looked like a leaf, was very important.

"Who are you?" Asked Wally politely.

"The name's Hopper, D I Hopper. That's Detective Inspector if you're unsure."

"Must work for Special Branch," thought Wally.

Hopper soon explained that there was some activity late last night and some teenagers had been messing with the garage doors to a property, but fortunately nobody had broken into the garage or caused any damage. However, Hopper was trying to obtain a description of the youths in case they came back.

"Thing is," said Hopper, "Would you believe it, those two German Shepherd dogs, 'Woofgang and Bach', slept through the whole incident."

"Call themselves guard dogs," laughed Sir Hillary "They're more like yard dogs."

With that D I Hopper flew away to continue his investigation.

On more than one occasion Woofgang and Bach could be heard yapping, morning and night!

One could often hear them yapping.
"Yap, Yap, Yap, Yap
We bark all day
And seldom nap."

Sometimes they could be heard barking during the night!

The one time that their barking would have been most welcome, they could be heard snoring their heads off!!

Typical!

Chapter 8
BARN A BEE

Spring and summer brought some welcome and some not so welcome, visitors to number1. Wally was busy working, tunnelling deeply into the soil. He popped his head up for a breather and could hear a strange buzzing noise.

"Buzz, buzz, buzz, buzz."

This character of yellow and black flew swiftly past. High and low, round and round...

"Buzz, buzz, buzz, buzz."

"Hello," greeted Wally.

"Good morning," he replied. "Don't recall seeing you here bee...fore?"

"I moved in a short time ago, my names Wally," he answered politely.

"I'm Barn a beeee." Barn a bee shook his head and his wings.

"I find it quite bee... wildering! Not a single flower in sight. Not even a daisy, a buttercup or even a dandelion anywhere. It's a travesty!! Call this a garden!"

Wally didn't quite understand why Barn a bee would need flowers. He knew nothing of nectar, the sugary fluid from plants, which attracts insects. Or that pollen from flowers is collected by bees, that this is important work for bees.

Wally didn't want to appear ignorant to the facts, so he said nothing.

Suddenly, WHACK!!

Barn a bee ducked and dodged and buzzed around faster and faster.

WHACK! WHACK!

One of the huge mans was chasing Barn a bee and attempting to hit him with a rolled up newspaper.

Wally was stunned. He had always thought the huge mans were kind to all the creatures in the garden.

After a few moments the huge man walked away.

"That's it!" Snorted Barn a bee. "Nobody whacks me and gets away with it!"

And with that he made a bee — line straight for the huge man. "Attack…..Charge!!!"

He zoomed across the garden, and skimmed the huge man on the nape of the neck. Panicking, the huge man gave a scream and hit himself across the head!!

Barn a bee laughed, "That'll teach you! You big bully!!"

"Are you alright?" Wally asked quite concerned.

"No problem. We bee's have to put up with this all the time. Bee… lieve it or not, they are more scared of me than I am of them." He stated quite proudly.

"How could this beee?" Pondered Wally, now beginning to speak like a bee! "The huge mans are much bigger than he is!"

"Well, I'm off. Number 3 has plenty of flowers to keep me busy — goodbye."

And with that he buzzed off and could be heard in the distance shouting…….

"Honey, I'm home!!"

19

Chapter 9
A Special Bond

It was a warm summer's morning and Wally was 'worm bathing' in the long green grass, beneath the scorching sun. Worms are cold blooded animals, so he soon decided just another five minutes and then he would tunnel deeply into the cool soil. Since his recent encounter with Barn a bee, his mind had been focused on the comments he'd made about number 3 and the flowers. For a moment Wally began to wonder if he had indeed been too hasty in leaving there. Perhaps the garden was much better now. After all Barn a bee was very keen to fly there.

He sighed and pondered, but his day dreaming soon came to a swift halt as the sound of 'screeching' became apparent.

The noise became louder and louder, it sounded nearer and nearer. Wally soon realised 'a machine' was getting much too close for comfort!!

"Take cover Wally!" Screamed Sir Hillary Cling On.

Wally appeared somewhat dazed, as this shiny silver roller skimmed past him.

Sir Hillary screamed again……….

"Now, Wally! Dig deep, into the mud. Quick! Not a second to lose!!"

Wally did indeed do so. Sir Hillary clung onto the fence with all of his might. Up and down the ferocious machine went, pushed by the huge man. Wally was soon to learn that he was Ian the Gardener! Fortunately Ian didn't mess about and the job was complete in minutes.

"Stay down!" Ordered Sir Hillary, as Ian raked and gathered all the grass together. He put the grass into bags and then left, closing the gate behind him.

"Coast clear!" Reassured Sir Hillary as he explained that now it was summer time, the gardener would come often and that machine would cut the grass. He gave Wally all the gory details.

"The blades are razor sharp, and no creature would stand a chance. Sliced into tiny pieces!!"

With that, Wally shuddered and curled his long body protectively, not wishing to be half the size!

Despite what people think, if a worm is cut in half it does not reproduce and become two worms! Earthworms, however, do have the ability to replace a lost segment and may be able to replace a lost tail.

Whatever!! Wally never ever wanted to find out!!

"Thank you Sir Hillary, you really are the dearest friend to me. I don't know what I would do without you!"

No doubt 'if' Wally had any eye's he would surely cry!

"Nonsense!" Said Sir Hillary, not one for all that emotional stuff, "Onwards and upwards, that's my motto!"

With that he set off for his challenge of the day, climbing the garden gate!

Wally did indeed love Sir Hillary; he was like a father to him. Someone he looked up to and admired. Now that special bond that Wally had with Sir Hillary is something he had never experienced before with anyone at number 3. If there ever were any reservations in having left that home, Sir Hillary had put those doubts out of Wally's mind.

Something good always comes out of a bad situation!

Chapter 10
THE EXPEDITION

Wally cheered as Sir Hillary climbed up the garden gate. Slowly but determined, he climbed higher and higher, leaving a trail of slime behind.

"Hurray!" Shouted Wally, as Sir Hillary reached a quarter of the way up the gate.

"Bang!"

Without warning the gate was flung open, and slammed against the fence. Then the gate slammed shut again.

It was that little monster, David, wheezy, from number 1!

"Bang!"

The gate was flung open a second time, then a third. It was the other two monsters Jacob and Darren. Mr Bossy and Mr Tumble!!

Then the three of them charged through the French doors.

(Ooh that word French again!)

Jacob could be heard asking if it was tea time! Always looking for food that one! Wally wiggled closer to the gate. "Sir Hillary, are you alright?"

Not a sound. Wally wiggled closer still. There was no sign of Sir Hillary.

"Oh my goodness!" Gasped Wally fearing the worst.

"He must have been flung off the gate!"

"Poor Sir Hillary." Wally was worried.

Suddenly "Boo!"

Wally nearly jumped out of his skin! Sir Hillary was stuck to the fence between number 1 and number 2!

"Blast those pesky kids!" Roared Sir Hillary, "I was just on my way to reaching the halfway mark! Never mind. Onwards and upwards!"

And off he went clinging bit by bit to the fence.

Wally finally recovered from the shock and gave a smile.

Nothing seemed to phase him.

Sir Hillary was indeed a true expeditionist!

Chapter 11
THE LOST QUAIL

Summer came and went and before long autumn had descended upon Victoria Way. The air was damp and it was a particularly cold day. Not that Wally minded, worms are cold blooded animals. Trees shed their leaves, carpeting the ground below. Maggie the Magpie was kept extremely busy, dusting and cleaning those branches.

"Hello Wally," said Sir Hillary. "Somewhat chilly today don't you………"

He was interrupted mid sentence, by a strange babbling sound. There stood, in front of the French doors, (Ooh that word again!) was what looked like a pure white furry round ball?

And it was babbling and dithering! A snowball that talked how strange!

"Stay low," said Sir Hillary as he edged forward to investigate.

"Well, I've never seen one of those around these parts before..."

"What, what is it?" Asked Wally anxiously.

"It's a Japanese Quail!!" Remarked Sir Hillary.

"Oh right. So what exactly is a Japanese Quail?"

"A type of bird, one of the Partridge family!" Informed Sir Hillary. He was so knowledgeable!

"Bird, Japan??" Thought Wally. "BIRD!"

With that he buried himself in the soil.

Sir Hillary watched and listened as the quail continued to babble and was dithering.

"Can you speak English?" Sir Hillary enquired.

With that the quail continued in his native tongue.

"Can't understand a single word he's saying," commented Sir Hillary, and just at that precise moment, one of the huge mans arrived and observed the bird.

The French door was opened, (Ooh that word!), and would you believe it! The Quail walked straight into the kitchen.

There was a height of activity in that kitchen and both Sir Hillary and Wally moved closer to find out what was happening. (Not that Wally could see, but Sir Hillary kept him up to speed by turning his hearing aid up to super sound!).

"He has some nerve! Must be a Kamikaze Quail! Walking straight into there! It is not unusual to see 'Quail' on the menu these days!"

"Oh!" Gasped Wally.

Although birds and Wally didn't really get along, he couldn't bear the thought of the Quail being served up with broccoli, carrots and new potatoes!!

Sir Hillary stood guard, and informed Wally of what the quail was doing!

"He's okay at the moment. Tottering around the kitchen."

"He's pooped all over the kitchen floor!" Giggled Sir Hillary.

"He's making his way under the table; he's taking up residence, looks like he's having a nap."

Sir Hillary shuffled down from the step.

"We can't help him now!"

Wally began to ask questions, he was quite excited to hear about the quail.

"Where's Japan?" Questioned Wally.

"A long, long, way, away," advised Sir Hillary. "One would probably go on an aeroplane and fly through the sky for many hours to get there!"

Wally tried to piece the jigsaw together. Bird? Fly? He'd heard there was a flight path at Birmingham Airport.

"The Quail must have landed there," thought Wally. "No wonder he was exhausted!"

"Blasted!" Cursed Sir Hillary, "They've closed the blinds!"

Wally and Sir Hillary saw nothing more of the Quail that night.

The following day, it was mid afternoon and the tempting aroma of roasted chicken? Wafted from the kitchen.

Sir Hillary turned to Wally.

"Surely they couldn't have? Could they?........

Chapter 12
TIME FOR BED

Autumn quickly passed and very soon winter set in. Some mornings the large garden stood frozen, at other times it seemed completely iced over. No fun for some of the animals. Forget me nut squirrel spent many days in the Tree Tops Hotels. During autumn she had been especially busy gathering a stock pile of nuts for winter.

Many of the animals went quiet, even the Invisible Cockerel! Although, his time clock seemed even more confused with the dark nights. Even the kids went quiet!! Well that was a relief!

"Well Wally," said Sir Hillary, "I will be moving to the bottom of the garden now……"

He began to move, snail pace, towards the playhouse.

"Are you leaving?" Asked Wally in a choky voice.

"No, not at all! Just settling down for a long winters nap. I won't see you for a while Wally, but look forward to the spring when we can have some fun together! Do take extra care while I'm away won't you. Time for bed. Night, night!"

"Oh!" Said Wally sadly as he watched Sir Hillary disappear behind the playhouse.

"Night, night, Sir Hillary. Hope you have a lovely Christmas or a 'silent night' at least!"

And with that, Wally tunnelled deeper through the frosted grass and into the soil below.

"See you in the spring," he whispered.

27

LaVergne, TN USA
18 March 2010
1734LVUK00002B